Daisy Dawson
and the
Big Freeze

Daisy Dawson

and the
Big Freeze

Steve Voake

illustrated by Jessica Meserve

CANDLEWICK PRESS

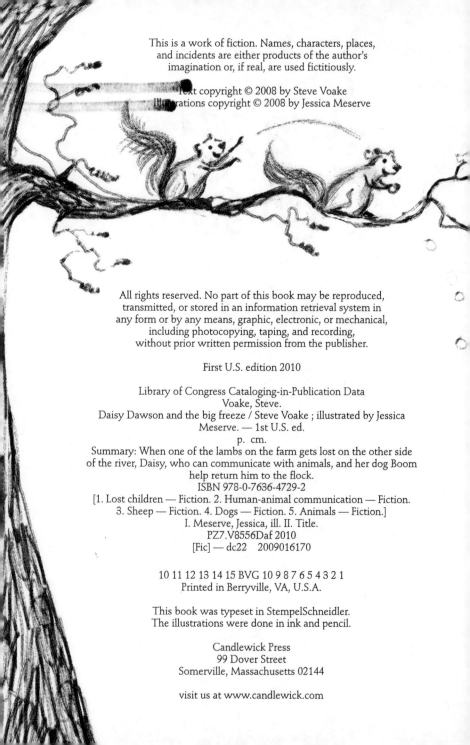

Text copyright © 2008 by Steve Voake
Illustrations copyright © 2008 by Jessica Meserve

First U.S. edition 2010

Library of Congress Cataloging-in-Publication Data
Voake, Steve.
Daisy Dawson and the big freeze / Steve Voake ; illustrated by Jessica
Meserve. — 1st U.S. ed.
p. cm.
Summary: When one of the lambs on the farm gets lost on the other side
of the river, Daisy, who can communicate with animals, and her dog Boom
help return him to the flock.
ISBN 978-0-7636-4729-2
[1. Lost children — Fiction. 2. Human-animal communication — Fiction.
3. Sheep — Fiction. 4. Dogs — Fiction. 5. Animals — Fiction.]
I. Meserve, Jessica, ill. II. Title.
PZ7.V8556Daf 2010
[Fic] — dc22   2009016170

10 11 12 13 14 15 BVG 10 9 8 7 6 5 4 3 2 1
Printed in Berryville, VA, U.S.A.

This book was typeset in StempelSchneidler.
The illustrations were done in ink and pencil.

Candlewick Press
99 Dover Street
Somerville, Massachusetts 02144

visit us at www.candlewick.com

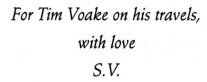

For Tim Voake on his travels,
with love
S.V.

Contents

Chapter 1

Stormy Skies

"You'll need to wrap up warm today," said Daisy's mom as she slid two pieces of hot buttered toast onto Daisy's plate. "They said on the news that it's getting much colder. Arctic winds coming in from the north, apparently."

Dad wandered into the kitchen with a mug of coffee in his hand.

"Arctic winds?" he said. "That'll be those penguins, flapping their wings together."

"There aren't any penguins in the Arctic," said Mom.

"Maybe it's polar bears then," suggested Daisy helpfully, "blowing on their paws to keep warm."

"Good point," said Dad. "Hadn't thought of that."

Daisy spread some honey on her toast and felt a tingle of excitement as she stared out at the gray blanket of clouds.

"Do you think it'll snow?" she asked.

"It might," said Dad. "You never know."

"If it does, those poor lambs are in for a shock," said Mom.

"Lambs?" asked Daisy. "What lambs?"

"The ones in the farmer's field. I saw them yesterday. They must have been born just a few days ago."

Daisy quickly finished off her toast and ran upstairs to brush her teeth.

"Someone's in a hurry this morning," said Dad when she came downstairs again. "Nothing to do with those lambs, I suppose?"

"Of course not," said Mom. "She just wants to get to school on time, don't you, sweetie?" She winked and handed Daisy a package wrapped in tin foil.

"Here," she said. "Just a little something for your friend."

Walking down the lane, Daisy felt the
cold wind blow through the hedges
and watched the catkins tremble on the
branches. When she reached the gate, she
cupped her mittens around her mouth and
called, "Boom? It's me, Daisy!"

A bloodhound appeared from around the
side of the barn, his ears flapping in the wind.

When he saw Daisy, he padded across the frosty grass toward her, sniffing the air as he went.

"Morning, Boom," said Daisy, wrapping her scarf more tightly around her neck. "How's life?"

Boom looked up and lifted one eyebrow.

"Life's cold," he said. "I had to drink from the river last night. The water trough's frozen solid." He shivered and looked up at the sky. "And I'm starting to know how that feels."

"Never mind," said Daisy. "I've got something here that'll warm you up."

"What's that?" asked Boom. "A packet of sunshine?"

"Not exactly," said Daisy, pulling out the package her mom had given her. "But it's the next best thing."

Feeling the heat seep through her mittens, she unwrapped the foil and produced two pieces of toast, dripping with melted butter.

Boom licked his lips as the steam rose into the cold winter air and woofed with delight as Daisy handed the toast through the gate.

"Have you seen the lambs yet?" she asked.

Boom held up a paw for a moment to show that his mouth was full, then said, "I was going to introduce you, as a matter of fact. Want to come over?"

"I'd love to," said Daisy, "but I don't think Miss Frink would be very pleased."

"I'll go to school instead, if you like," said Boom. "Just give me your backpack and Miss

Frink will never know the difference."

Daisy smiled. "I think the ears might give you away," she said. "That and the fact that you're a dog."

"I *am*?" said Boom, pretending to be surprised. "Well, that explains the strange looks at the hairdresser's."

He laughed, then coughed, then accidentally inhaled the last bite of his toast and Daisy had to climb over the gate to pat him on the back.

"Thanks," he said. "You can stop now."

"Oh, right," said Daisy. "Sorry."

"Why don't you pop over and see the lambs on your way home from school?" suggested Boom when he'd gotten his breath back. "I'll come with you, if you like."

"It's a date," said Daisy happily. Then she heard the sound of the school bell ringing and jumped down from the gate. "Got to go, Boom," she said. "See you later!"

* * *

Miss Frink was busy reviewing everyone's book choice when Daisy arrived, so she didn't notice that Daisy was late.

"That's all very well," she told Bobby Mitchell, who was clutching a magazine with pictures of trucks on the front, "but it's not a reading book, Bobby."

As Bobby went off to search the bookshelves again, Daisy remembered a job she was supposed to do.

"Miss Frink?" she asked when the teacher had finished reviewing Jessica Brinton's book choice. "Do you want me to clean out the gerbils' cage?"

Miss Frink peered over the top of her glasses. "That depends, Daisy. Are you a Tidy Monitor?"

"Yes, Miss Frink," said Daisy, pointing at her badge with a picture of a dustpan and brush on it.

Miss Frink looked at her watch. "Well, all right, then. But don't be too long about it."

As Daisy picked up the gerbils' cage, Furball leaped up onto his hind legs and put his paws out as if trying to balance on a tightrope.

"Whaaay," he said, sliding about in the sawdust as Daisy carried the cage out into the hallway, where there was a sink and a long bench. "Whoaah!"

"Having fun?" she asked, at which point

he fell over and banged his head on the water dish.

"Not anymore," he said.

There was a rustle from the corner of the cage and Burble emerged, padding sleepily across the sawdust.

"Morning, Daisy D," she said. "What's going on?"

"I'm cleaning your cage out," said Daisy.

"Ooh, that's nice of you," said Furball. "I love the smell of fresh sawdust in the morning. Besides, Burble makes such a mess of the place."

"Hey," said Burble, "I think we all know who drops their sunflower seeds all over the place."

Daisy opened the top of the cage and put her hand in. "OK. Who's first?"

"Me, me, me!" cried Furball, hopping onto Daisy's palm. Then, remembering his manners, he turned to Burble and added, "Unless you want to?"

"No, it's all right," said Burble. "I know how much you love this part."

"It's true!" agreed Furball, clapping his paws together. "I do!"

As Daisy lifted him into the air, Furball stood on his hind legs and called "Going up!" as if he were riding in an elevator. Then, as Daisy set him down again, he said, "Bing-bong," made the sound of doors opening, and stepped out onto the bench. "First floor for paint," he said, looking around. "Paint,

margarine containers, and old newspaper."

"Don't forget sawdust," said Daisy, reaching into the cupboard and taking out a bag.

"Sawdust too?" replied Furball, pressing his paws together. "Well, tie my tail to a tomcat. This place has *everything*!"

"He'll calm down in a minute," said Burble as Daisy lifted her gently out of the cage. "He's always like this first thing in the morning."

"Hey, wait!" said Furball. "What's *that*?"

"What now?" asked Burble. "A paintbrush, maybe? A bunch of pencils?"

"No," squeaked Furball, jumping up and down and waving his paw in the direction of the window. "Look! Out *there*!"

Daisy followed his gaze, and her eyes
widened in surprise. Outside, the air was
filled with a flurry of thick white flakes,
whirling and fluttering as they tumbled from
the sky.

"Oh," she gasped in delight. "It's snowing!"

Chapter 2

Snowballs

After an assembly (where Mr. Blake told them that If People Are Sensible, Snow Can Be Fun), Daisy slipped Burble and Furball into her coat pockets and hurried down the hallway toward the playground.

"Are we there yet?" asked Furball in a muffled voice. "Are we there yet?"

"Almost," said Daisy. "Now then, you two. It's pretty cold out there, so I don't think you should be out for long."

Furball popped his head out of Daisy's

pocket and asked, "What do you mean, cold?" when the doors swung open and a gust of wind came howling down the hallway.

"Holy moly," he gasped, diving back into the warmth of Daisy's pocket. "I've frozen my nozen!"

Daisy stepped out through the doors and felt the snow crunch beneath her feet.

"Hey, Daisy Dawson!" called a voice. "Want some breakfast?" Daisy glanced around to see Bobby Mitchell throw a snowball, but she quickly ducked her head and the snowball thudded harmlessly into the wall.

Without stopping to think, she scooped
up a handful of snow and threw it with
such speed that it exploded right in the
middle of Bobby Mitchell's forehead. As
he fell backward into the snow, Daisy
ran giggling around the corner to the side
playground, which was empty of children.
Looking down the hill toward the town
with its roofs all dusted with snow, she saw
something moving and realized it was a
squirrel, waving at her through the fence.

"Cyril!" she called, stamping a trail of
snowy footprints across the playground.
"What are you doing here?"

"Good morning, Daisy," said Cyril. "Hazel and Conker wanted to take a walk, so I thought we'd come over and say hello."

Daisy waved at the two young squirrels, who were busy building something out of snow. "Hello, you two. What are you up to?"

"We're making a snow squirrel," replied Conker, banging his paws together. "Right, Haze?"

"Trying to," said Hazel. "But the tail keeps falling off." She stopped, and stared at Daisy through the fence. "Ooh, you're in a cage! Do they put you in it every day?"

Daisy smiled. "It's not a cage. It's just a fence to make sure that everyone stays in the right place."

"Looks like a cage to me," said Conker. "What's the food like?"

"Not bad," said a small voice, "except for the sawdust."

"Who said that?" Conker asked, looking around.

"I did," said Furball, popping his head out of Daisy's pocket. "Who said 'Who said that?'"

"Me!" squeaked Conker excitedly. "I said 'Who said that?'! But who said 'Who said who said that?'"

Hazel giggled. "My brain hurts," she said, putting her paws over her eyes.

Daisy crouched down and took Burble and Furball out of her pocket. As the gerbils gazed in wonder at the snowy scene, Hazel and Conker stuck their noses through the wire fence.

"Oh, looook!" said Hazel. "Aren't they sweet?"

"You're very *small* squirrels," said Conker, looking them up and down. "You should probably eat more nuts. We've got lots stashed away in the old—"

"Conker!" said Cyril sharply. "A squirrel *never*

gives away the location of his winter store!"

"Oops," said Conker, looking up at Daisy.

"Don't worry," Daisy whispered. "I won't tell."

"Anyway, we're not squirrels," said Furball. "We're gerbils. We live in the desert."

"No, we don't," said Burble. "We live in that classroom over there."

"It's *kind* of a desert," said Furball.

"Oh?" said Burble. "In what way?"

"Well," said Furball, rubbing his paws together, "it's warm. And also . . . there's no snow in it."

"Hmm," said Burble. "Or sand. Or camels."

"D'you know, I never thought of that," said Furball. "I wonder where they went?"

"Do you want to come and play?" asked Hazel, changing the subject. "We're going slippy-slidey in a minute, aren't we, Uncle Cyril?"

Cyril gave Daisy a look that suggested that slippy-slidey wasn't at the top of his to-do list.

"Perhaps," he said. "We'll see."

"That means yes," explained Conker.

Burble and Furball looked at Daisy. "Well, Daisy. What d'you say?"

Daisy thought for a moment. "I don't know," she said cautiously. "The field's very big, and you're very small."

"But just think about it," Conker said. "The world is even bigger. But that doesn't stop them from opening your cage at the end of the day, does it?"

"That's different," said Daisy.

She was about to explain *why* it was different when she suddenly realized that maybe it wasn't. And besides, it wasn't every day that a pair of school gerbils got to play slippy-slidey with squirrels.

"All right," she said. "But be careful."

"Yay!" cried Burble and Furball together.

"Climb," said Conker, pressing up against the fence. With an excited squeak, Furball squeezed through and onto his head.

"Hold on to my ears," said Conker, "and get set for the ride of your life!"

"Woah!" exclaimed Furball. "This is so cool!"

Hazel put her head down so that Burble could climb on, and soon both gerbils were sitting on the squirrels' heads, clutching their ears as if they were motorcycle handlebars.

"Uh-oh," giggled Burble. "Where are the brakes?"

"Brakes?" replied Conker. "Who needs brakes?" He looked at Hazel, and she nodded. Then they ran at top speed toward the slope of the hill.

"Waaaaaah!" cried Burble and Furball. "Waaaaaaaaaaay!"

Hazel and Conker threw themselves

onto their tummies, and Daisy heard the squeals and shrieks of excitement fade as they rocketed away down the hill. She saw the tiny figures of Burble and Furball desperately hanging on to the squirrels' ears as they shot over a bump and launched into the air like a couple of furry missiles before slamming into a snowdrift at the bottom.

"Oh dear," said Cyril, looking away. "Do you think they're all right?"

"I think so," said Daisy. "Look."

Hazel
and Conker
were staggering to
their feet and digging
in the snow with their paws.
When they found Burble and Furball,
they plonked them back on their heads,
waved, and began scampering back up the
hill again.

"Wow!" cried Conker when he reached
the top. "That was fantastic! Can we do it
again?"

Daisy saw that snow had melted into
the gerbils' fur and they looked very wet
and bedraggled. They were both shivering,
and she remembered that they were more
suited to life in the desert. "Come on, you

two," she said. "I think we'd better get you back inside."

"Aw, do we *have* to?" Furball protested. But when she saw how quickly they jumped through the fence and onto her hand, Daisy guessed both gerbils would be glad to be back in their comfortable cage again. She had just put them into her pockets when she heard something behind her and turned to see Bobby Mitchell grinning and clutching a large snowball.

"Found you!" he shouted triumphantly. "I'll get you this time!"

He flung the snowball and charged back around the corner. Daisy stepped aside, and the snowball flew past and hit Conker full in the face. The force of the impact lifted the small squirrel clean off his feet and sent him flying backward into the snow.

"Oh, my goodness!" exclaimed Daisy. "Conker, are you all right?"

Conker lay still for a few moments, stunned by the impact, then he staggered to his feet, shook snow from his fur and clapped his paws together.

"Awesome!" he squeaked. "Totally awesome!"

Hazel smiled. "Looks like I got my snow squirrel after all."

Chapter 3

Lambs

"It must be strange for the lambs, don't you think?" asked Daisy as she walked with Boom across the snowy field. "Being born into a world that's so white and cold?"

"I suppose they don't know anything else," said Boom. "They've never tasted grass or felt the sun's warmth or seen flower petals fluttering in the breeze. They don't know how sweet the earth smells after a rain shower."

"But just think," said Daisy, "they have all those wonderful things to look forward to."

"Unfortunately," sniffed Boom, "right now most of them are hidden beneath the snow."

"Well, here's one that isn't," said Daisy. She pulled a cookie from her pocket and broke it in two, giving one half to Boom and popping the other half in her mouth.

They made their way around the back of the barn and past the old pigpens until they came to the next field. Boom squeezed through the gate and waited for Daisy to climb over. As she jumped down into the snow, she looked up and saw a flock of sheep gathered around some bales of hay.

"Hey, Shirelle!" called Boom as snowflakes swirled around them. "I've brought someone to meet you."

A large ewe turned and eyed Daisy suspiciously.

"Hello," said Daisy, holding out her hand. She quickly dropped it again when she realized that trying to shake hands with a

sheep was probably not the best approach. "I'm Daisy Dawson, and I'm very pleased to meet you."

Shirelle looked at Boom. "Am I hearing things," she asked, "or did the little two-leggedy say she was pleased to meet me?"

"Daisy can talk to all of us," explained Boom in his deep, quiet voice. "And what's more, she can understand what we're saying too."

Shirelle the sheep turned and nodded approvingly at Daisy. "Well, aren't you precious?" she said. "And such good manners. Ooh, I could just eat you up. But don't worry, I'm a vegetarian."

"Mommy!" bleated a little voice from behind her. "Mommy! Mommy!"

"Excuse me," said Shirelle, turning to look at the little white lamb struggling through the snow toward her. "What is it, Lillian my lambkin? What's wrong?"

"It's Woolverton," said Lillian in a small, wavery voice. "He's wandered off again."

"Oh, *no!*" said Shirelle. "Didn't I just tell him to stay with us?" She trotted over to where the lambs were gathered and stared out across the snowy fields.

"Woolverton!" she called, and immediately all the lambs began bleating, "Woolverton! Woolverton! WOOLVERTON!"

"Is that him?" Daisy whispered as a dark shape came bounding across the snow toward them. "He's very fast."

"No," said Boom. "That's Ricky Round-Up."

The shape skidded to a halt in front of them, and Daisy saw that it was a young

(and very out of breath) sheepdog.

"I know where he is, I know where he is," he panted.

"Well," said Shirelle, "perhaps telling us would be a start."

Ricky held up a paw to show that he was getting his breath back. "I'll give you three guesses."

"Down by the river?" asked Boom.

"Bull's-eye, big fella," said Ricky. "Got it on the first try."

"How many times have I told him that sheep do *not* wander off on their own?" said Shirelle angrily. "A sheep must stay with the flock. It's the way of things. Always has been, always will be."

"Not this time," said Ricky. He winked at one of the young lambs, who giggled and nearly choked on a mouthful of hay.

"Don't be too hard on him, Shirelle," said Boom. "He just wants to find out more about the world."

"That's all very well," sniffed Shirelle, "but the world can be a dangerous place. Some parts don't even have any hay in them. Can you *imagine*?"

"We'll go and look for him, if you like," Daisy offered.

"You're very kind," replied Shirelle, "but I think that is actually *someone else's* job."

Ricky was busy showing the lambs how to make paw prints in the snow, but when he heard this, he sat up straight and wagged his tail.

"Absolutely, ma'am. And I just want to say how much I appreciate the rest of you young'uns staying together like this. Makes my job a whole lot easier."

As he ran off across the fields, the lambs tried making prints in the snow.

"They're not the same," complained Lillian after a few attempts. "They're too . . . hoofy looking. I wish I had paws like Ricky."

"But then you'd be a dog-sheep too," said her brother Lionel.

"Sheepdog," corrected Shirelle.

"Whatever," said Lionel.

"Can you make prints, Daisy?" Lillian asked shyly.

"Well, let me see," said Daisy.

She stepped forward and pressed her foot into the snow,

then stepped back to reveal
the print of her snow boot.

"Whoa!" exclaimed Lionel.
"Nice paws!"

"Do more, do more!" bleated
the lambs. But before Daisy
could oblige, Ricky reappeared
with a small damp lamb
scampering behind him.

"The river spoke to me!" cried the
lamb, jumping up and down
enthusiastically. "It said blurble-urble,
wishety-woshety, splishety-sploshety
splash!"

"Woolverton!" scolded Shirelle. "How
many times have I told you? You are *not*
to go wandering off like that, d'you hear
me?"

Woolverton stared at the ground,
unable to meet his mother's gaze.
Then, summoning up all

his courage, he looked up and said, "But I want to know what's out there. I want to see the world."

"You're not allowed to cross the river," said Ricky. "You're a sheep and you have to act like all the others. If you start thinking for yourself, it'll cause no end of trouble. Take it from me, the other side of the river is bad. It takes things away from you. It takes them away and never gives them back!"

Ricky shook his head sadly before sprinting

across the fields toward the lights of the distant farmhouse.

"Now look what you've done," said Shirelle. "You've gone and upset Ricky!"

"But I didn't mean to," said Woolverton softly.

"Why's Ricky so worried about the other side of the river?" Daisy asked.

"Because it's no place for us sheep to be poking our noses," said Shirelle. "And if animals start going where they have no business going, then there's no telling what might happen."

Daisy was about to explain that she'd already been there and that no one had gotten hurt (except for Hazel falling in the river) when she caught Boom's eye and noticed that he was shaking his head.

"I'll tell you later," he whispered.

"Come on, everyone," said Shirelle as the

wind picked up and snow whirled around in a flurry of white. "Let's huddle. Do you want to join us, Daisy dear?"

Daisy realized that she should be getting home. "I'd love to, but my mom will be back from work soon and I don't want her to worry."

"Ah, you're a good girl and no mistake," said Shirelle. "Did you hear that, Woolverton? She doesn't want her mother to worry!"

"I heard," said Woolverton miserably, which made Daisy wish she'd kept quiet.

"Off you go then, dear," said Shirelle. "But come back and see us soon."

"I will," said Daisy. "I promise."

As she and Boom walked across the fields, the sound of Shirelle's singing floated up through the frosty air:

Sometimes the sun shines

Sometimes it rains

Sometimes the wind blows

Up and down the lanes.

Sometimes the snow falls soft upon our heads

And you and I sleep silently

In our little beds. . . .

"Tell me about Ricky," said Daisy. "What happened to him?"

"Well," said Boom, "when he was a young pup, Ricky used to get lonely when everyone went off to work, so the farmer's wife bought him a rubber ball to play with. Ricky *loved* that little red ball. He used to carry it everywhere with him, from first thing in the morning until last thing at night. And when he went to bed, the ball would always be right there beside him."

"But what's that got to do with the woods?" asked Daisy.

"One morning," Boom went on, "the farmer's wife had a friend visiting and they decided to go for a walk in the woods. Ricky went with them, taking his ball of course, and the friend threw it for Ricky to fetch. Ricky ran happily around the field, chasing after his ball, but when they crossed the bridge into the woods, it disappeared into the trees, never to be seen again."

"Oh, no," said Daisy. "Was he really upset?"

"Heartbroken. That ball meant so much to him, you see. Ever since then he's refused to cross the bridge into the woods, because he believes it will take something else away from him."

"Poor Ricky," said Daisy as they reached the gate. "Is that why he got mad at Woolverton?"

Boom looked at her thoughtfully. "I think sometimes when you've lost something you love, you can't help worrying that it will happen again."

"I know," said Daisy, tapping the silver name tag on Boom's collar and kissing him on the nose. "That's why I bought you this, remember?"

Chapter 4

Cool for Cats

The next morning was Saturday, and when Daisy pulled back her curtains, she saw that there had been another heavy snowfall during the night. The fields were white, and the light was so crisp and clear that the whole world seemed brand new.

After breakfast, she quickly pulled on her boots and mittens before heading for the door.

"Just off to see Boom," she called. "We're going to see the lambs again today."

Daisy's mom popped her head around the door and smiled. "He's a good friend to you, isn't he?"

"Who? Boom?"

"Yes. It's funny, but whenever I see you with him I feel as if he's looking after you and keeping you safe. The other day I was watching you together and the way you were smiling and nodding your head, I could have sworn you were having a conversation!"

"He was probably telling me how cold he was," replied Daisy. "He had to drink from the river the other night."

Mom chuckled. "You always did have a lively imagination, Daisy Dawson," she said.

For a moment, Daisy was tempted to try to explain, but then she remembered that grown-ups' lives were already quite complicated enough.

Meadowsweet the mare was standing at the edge of the field, snuffling at a bale of hay. When she saw Daisy, she whinnied happily and stamped her feet.

"Well, if it isn't my favorite girl," she said, leaning over the gate and nuzzling Daisy's neck.

"Aren't you freezing?" asked Daisy, stroking the mare's nose.

"Not anymore," replied Meadowsweet. "I've just been for a gallop around the field and it warmed me right up."

"Simple things for simple minds," said a husky voice.

Daisy turned to see a sleek gray cat sitting on the fence, licking a paw.

"Good morning, Trixie," said Meadowsweet.

"Is it?" replied Trixie.

"Oh, dear," said Daisy, winking at Meadowsweet. "Someone's grumpy this morning."

"I am not grumpy," replied Trixie haughtily. "I merely find it hard to see what can be good about a morning that is packed full of snow and very little else."

"Well, I think it's beautiful," said Meadowsweet.

"So do I," said Daisy. "I mean, just look at it, Trixie!"

"I'm looking," replied Trixie, "but I'm not seeing. And what I'm particularly not seeing are any warm fires or comfortable armchairs to curl up in. Just field after field of cold, wet snow. Hardly fall-off-the-fence fantastic, is it?"

Daisy frowned. "Have you ever done that?" she asked.

Trixie examined her paw. "Done what?"

"Fallen off a fence."

Trixie looked at Daisy disdainfully. "That would be dogs you're thinking of."

Then, as if to demonstrate her perfect balance, she began strolling elegantly along the wooden rail. "Poise," she purred, "is the name of the game. Some of us have it . . . and some of us don't."

"Careful now, Trixie," said Meadowsweet. "After all, you know what they say. Pride comes before a fall."

"Well, whoever came up with that piece of nonsense obviously knew nothing about cats."

At that moment a snowball flew past Daisy's ear and hit Trixie with a loud *thump,* sending her yowling sideways into a pile of snow.

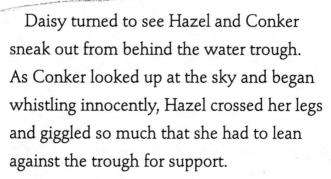

Daisy turned to see Hazel and Conker sneak out from behind the water trough. As Conker looked up at the sky and began whistling innocently, Hazel crossed her legs and giggled so much that she had to lean against the trough for support.

"Conker!" said Daisy, trying hard not to laugh.

Conker grinned and clasped his paws together, pretending to be surprised. "Oh, no," he said, "don't tell me my snowball hit a cat or something. Now I feel just *awful*."

At this, Hazel slid down into the snow, squeaking with laughter.

"I must say," said Trixie as she emerged from the snow and shook herself, "that was a magnificent shot. You really have good aim."

Hazel stopped laughing and looked at Trixie in amazement. "Aren't you angry?"

"Angry?" purred Trixie. "Of course not. Actually, I've always enjoyed games myself. I have to say though, my absolute favorite is the stone clap. Watch this."

As they all looked on, Trixie picked up a small stone, threw it up into the air, and clapped her paws five times before catching it again.

"Wow," said Conker. "That's cool!"

"You're most kind," replied Trixie,

"although, considering the way you threw that snowball, I think you could do even better."

"Me?" asked Conker.

"Mmm-hmm," said Trixie. "You obviously have a gift for these things." She batted the stone to Conker with her paw, and he caught it in midair.

"You see?" said Trixie. "Such talent."

The others watched as Conker stood beneath the tree and threw the stone into the air, clapping three times before catching it again.

"Not bad," said Trixie. "But if you want to beat my record you'll have to throw it much higher than that."

"Easy-peasy," said Conker. "Here goes!" He threw the stone high into the old oak tree, and there was a sudden, sharp crack as it struck a branch.

"Uh-oh," said Hazel.

As Conker clapped furiously, a thick layer of snow slid off the branch and plummeted down onto his head, burying him beneath it with a loud *flump!*

There was silence for a few seconds, then Conker popped his head out of the snow, a dazed expression on his face. Trixie shook her head. "Oh, no," she purred. "Don't tell me the snow fell on the squirrel. Oh, now I feel just *awful*." And with that, she turned and padded away up the lane with her head and tail high in the air.

Conker dug himself out of the snow and looked around expectantly. "Did I win?" he asked.

At that moment, the sound of bleating drifted over from the sheep's field and Boom appeared, ears pricked up to listen. "Something's wrong," he said.

"Hello, Boom," said Daisy. "What do you mean? Are the lambs in trouble?"

"I think we'd better go and find out," he said.

Chapter 5
Lost

When they reached the sheep's field, Daisy could see Shirelle running around, checking each of the lambs in turn.

"Are you sure he's not here?" she bleated. "Are you sure no one's seen him?"

"What is it, Shirelle?" asked Daisy. "What's the matter?"

"It's Woolverton! He's disappeared and we can't find him anywhere!"

"What about Ricky?" asked Boom.

"Ricky won't be here until later. He's gone

to help the farmer with one of his other flocks. Oh, what am I going to do?"

"Well," said Boom, looking at a trail of hoofprints leading down to the river. "I think we had better start by following these."

"Oh, no," Daisy whispered. "You don't think . . . ?"

Boom nodded. "I'm afraid I do."

Shirelle came as far as the bridge, but when she saw how the hoofprints crossed over and disappeared into the woods, she sat down in the snow and wept.

"Ricky was right!" she cried. "The woods take away the things we love! And now it's taken Woolverton too!"

"Don't worry," said Daisy determinedly. "We'll find him."

"But it's not safe!" protested Shirelle. "We might lose you as well."

"You won't. We'll be back before you know it," Daisy reassured her.

But as they crossed the bridge, Daisy whispered, "It's not true, is it, Boom? About the woods taking away the things we love?"

"Maybe not," replied Boom. "But it tried to take you away once, remember?"

Daisy thought about the last time they'd been in the woods, when she'd nearly drowned trying to save Hazel, and Boom had come to her rescue.

"Let's stay out of the water this time, okay?" she said.

"That," said Boom, "is a very good idea."

As they walked farther into the woods, the sky darkened, and the wind shook the trees so that ice pattered down onto the woodland floor. Suddenly the air was filled with thick flakes of snow, swirling and dancing all around them.

They stopped by a fallen tree, which reminded Daisy of a chocolate log dusted with powdered sugar, just like the ones her mother brought home at Christmas. She thought of the lighted windows, the warm fire burning in the fireplace and, as the snow continued to fall all around her, she wished—just for a moment—that she was safe and warm in her own little house. But then she remembered that Woolverton was lost, and she knew she couldn't be happy until he was home again.

But the woods were deep, and the snow had covered the last of his tracks. How would they ever find him?

"Look," whispered Boom. "Over there. Behind the trees."

Daisy followed Boom's gaze and saw something moving in the shadows.

"Woolverton?" she called. "Woolverton, is that you?"

At the sound of Daisy's voice, whatever it was stopped moving and began to speak in a slow, serious voice.

"Who are you? What do you want here?"

"Please," said Daisy uncertainly. "We're looking for Woolverton. He's a young lamb, and his mother is worried about him. Do you know where we might find him?"

There was a rustle of branches and then, to Daisy's surprise, a large badger trotted out into the clearing. He looked Daisy up and down for a few moments before turning to look at Boom.

"She speaks the language of the forest," he said warily. "What trickery is this?"

"There's no trickery," Boom replied. "Daisy's gift is born out of kindness."

"Did you say Daisy?"said the badger. He turned to look at her. "Are you Daisy Dawson?"

"Yes," said Daisy. "How did you know?"

"The otters often speak of you," replied the badger. "But I always thought they were just making up stories."

Daisy thought back to the hot

afternoon she'd spent swimming with
Dampsy and Spray in the otters' pool. The
summer seemed a long time ago now.

"The stories were true," said Boom, "and
you have nothing to fear."

"I can see she has a good heart," replied
the badger. "But this is no place for a human
cub. The wind grows wild and the trees are
all a-shiver. You must return by the path that
brought you here."

"No!" said Daisy. "Not yet. Not without
Woolverton."

The badger stared at her for a long moment.
"I see you will not be put off," he said. "Your
courage matches your kindness. I'm afraid
I cannot come with you, as I must return
to my family. But this morning I heard a
strange tale that may be of some use to
you. The birds were twittering in their usual
way, and I paid them little attention. But
then I heard a wren telling some robins that

she had seen a magical talking thorn bush in the middle of the woods."

"A magical talking *thorn bush*?" repeated Boom.

"That's what they said. I didn't believe them at first. But now I'm not so sure."

"Why?" asked Daisy.

"Because a few minutes ago, I didn't believe in a magical talking girl either," said the badger.

"Oh," said Daisy. "I see what you mean."

"This thorn bush," Boom went on, "do you think it might help us?"

The badger looked thoughtful. "All I know is, there's enough magic in this world for those who want to look for it." And with that, he turned and disappeared into the woods.

"How strange," said Daisy. "It's worth a try though, don't you think?"

* * *

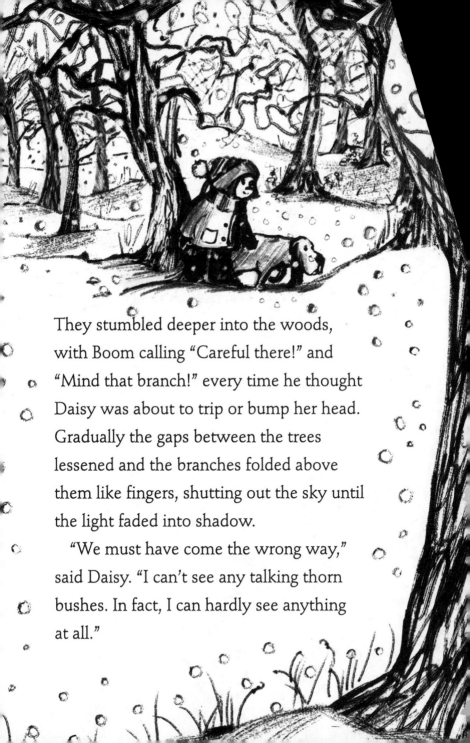

They stumbled deeper into the woods,
with Boom calling "Careful there!" and
"Mind that branch!" every time he thought
Daisy was about to trip or bump her head.
Gradually the gaps between the trees
lessened and the branches folded above
them like fingers, shutting out the sky until
the light faded into shadow.

"We must have come the wrong way,"
said Daisy. "I can't see any talking thorn
bushes. In fact, I can hardly see anything
at all."

She saw that Boom had
stopped and was sitting in the
snow with his head to one side.
"What is it?" she asked.
"Listen," said Boom.
At first all she could hear was the
sound of the wind. But then, as she
listened more carefully, she heard a faint
mumbling sound.
"Look!" she cried. "Over there!"
Beyond the trunk of an old beech tree
was a thick tangle of brambles. As
Daisy watched, the bush began
to tremble.
"That must be it,"
whispered Boom. "The
magical thorn
bush!"

"Maybe we should ask it questions,"
Daisy suggested, moving a little closer.
"Excuse me, Thorn Bush, but can you talk?"

"Ye-es," said the thorn bush in a quivery
voice.

Daisy turned back to Boom and put
a hand up to the side of her mouth.
"It can talk!" she whispered.

Boom came over to investigate.

"Are you real?" the thorn bush
asked. "Or am I just hearing things?"

"Of course I'm real," said Daisy.
"The question is, are you?"

"I think so," said the thorn bush.
"But to be honest, I'm not
sure anymore."

Boom began to sniff the air, and Daisy noticed that there was a twinkle in his eye.

"Sing us a song," he said.

"A song?" asked the thorn bush.

"Yes," said Boom. "Anything you like."

"Boom," said Daisy, "I don't think—"

"Shh!" said Boom. "Just listen."

So Daisy listened.

And very quietly, the thorn bush began to sing:

Sometimes the sun shines
Sometimes it rains
Sometimes the wind blows
Up and down the lanes.
Sometimes the snow falls soft upon our heads
And you and I sleep silently
In our little beds. . . .

Chapter 6

Found

When they reached the river about half an hour later, Daisy saw Ricky sitting alone on the other side of the bridge. A thin layer of snow had settled on the top of his head, and he looked so sad that Daisy ran across to comfort him.

"Ricky!" she cried, putting her arms around him. "What's the matter?"

"I lost one of my sheep," said Ricky, hanging his head, "and that's something a sheepdog should never do."

"Well," said Daisy, "I happen to know something that will make you feel much better."

She put her hands on either side of his head and turned it so that he was facing the bridge. "Now look over there and tell me what you see."

Ricky squinted through the falling snow. "I see Boom," he said, "coming over the bridge."

"OK," said Daisy. "Anyone else?"

Ricky looked again. He sat up straight and whimpered. His tail went *thump, thump, thump* on the snow.

Then with a yelp of joy he took off across
the snow, barking, "Woolverton! Woolverton!
WOOLVERTON!"

As the four of them walked back up the hill,
Daisy said, "Oh, wait. We almost forgot."

The others stopped and looked at her.

"What did we forget?" asked Ricky.

"We forgot to tell you the reason Woolverton
went into the woods in the first place."

Ricky looked at Woolverton. "Why *did* you
go?"

Woolverton stared at the ground. "You were
sad," he said softly, "so I went to try to find
the thing you lost."

"You went over the bridge to look for my
ball?" asked Ricky. "You did that for me?"

Woolverton nodded shyly.

"Well, you know what?" said Ricky. "I loved that ball, but if I had to choose between the ball and you, I'd choose you every time, little fella."

"Actually," said Woolverton, "you don't have to."

"What d'you mean?" asked Ricky, puzzled.

"You don't have to choose," said Woolverton.

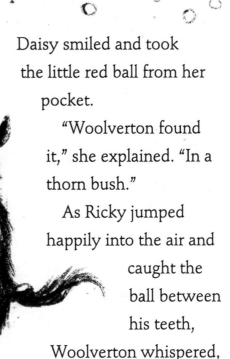

Daisy smiled and took the little red ball from her pocket.

"Woolverton found it," she explained. "In a thorn bush."

As Ricky jumped happily into the air and caught the ball between his teeth, Woolverton whispered, "I knew it wasn't lost, Daisy. I knew that if I kept on searching I would find it in the end."

Daisy knelt down next to him and put her arms around his neck. "That's funny," she said. "Because I thought the exact same thing about you."

* * *

71

When she got home, Daisy took a long bath. It had been an exhausting day, and it was a wonderful feeling to stop and do nothing for a while. Afterward, she sat in the big armchair with a plate of hot buttered toast and warmed her feet in front of the fire.

"You played in the snow for hours," said Mom, placing a mug of hot chocolate on the little wooden table next to Daisy's chair. "Did you find the lambs all right?"

"We did," said Daisy. "Although one of them got lost for a while. But Boom helped me find him again."

"Oh," said Mom. "I didn't know Boom was a sheepdog."

"He's not," Daisy explained as Dad came in with a basket of logs. "But the real sheepdog was busy, so we decided to help out for a while."

"Good for you," said Dad, putting another log on the fire. "I hope he was grateful."

Daisy smiled. "Oh, he was," she said. "He definitely was."

As her eyes began to close, she felt Dad gather her up in his arms and whisper, "Come on, tired girl. That's enough excitement for one day."

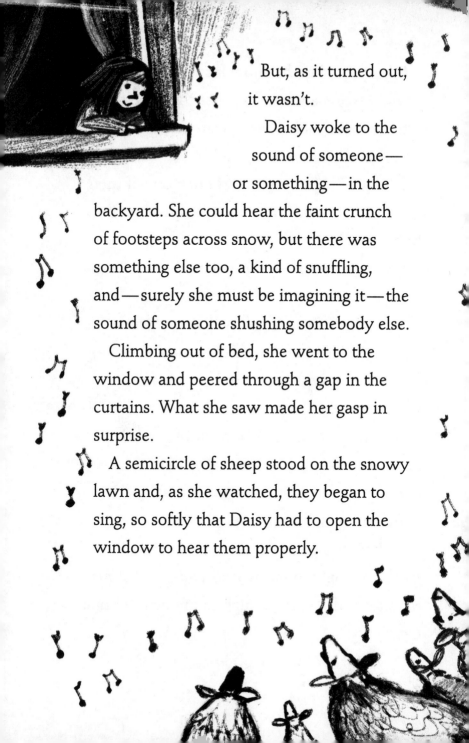

But, as it turned out, it wasn't.

Daisy woke to the sound of someone — or something — in the backyard. She could hear the faint crunch of footsteps across snow, but there was something else too, a kind of snuffling, and — surely she must be imagining it — the sound of someone shushing somebody else.

Climbing out of bed, she went to the window and peered through a gap in the curtains. What she saw made her gasp in surprise.

A semicircle of sheep stood on the snowy lawn and, as she watched, they began to sing, so softly that Daisy had to open the window to hear them properly.

Now the moon is in the treetops
Shining stars are clear and bright
Snow falls over fields and rooftops
On this cold and wintry night.

Sadness has been turned around
And all our darkness turned to light
What was lost has now been found
And Daisy Dawson made it right.

Then all the sheep turned their faces up to the window and began singing in harmony:

May your heart be always true
And may the world be good to you.
Daisy Dawson, friend of sheep,
You're a friend we'll always keep.

As they moved their heads in time to the tune, Daisy leaned on the windowsill and listened until the last note faded away. Then, as she clapped her hands together, Shirelle called, "Come down, Daisy! Come down and see us!"

Quickly closing the window, Daisy pulled on her robe and slippers and tiptoed down the stairs. When she opened the door into the backyard, all the sheep got into a circle and Daisy noticed that Boom was waiting by the back gate.

"Hello, Boom," she whispered as he

wandered over. "Did they sing to you too?"

Boom nodded. "Woke me up, as a matter of fact. But it was very nice all the same."

Woolverton stepped forward, and Daisy saw that he was carrying something in his mouth. When he dropped it in the snow, she saw that it was a ball of wool.

Woolverton held one end in his mouth and rolled the ball to Daisy so that a line of wool lay across the snow between them.

"Hold on to your piece," he whispered, "and roll the ball to Boom."

Puzzled, Daisy rolled the ball of wool to Boom so that there were now two lines in the snow, one between her and Woolverton, and one between her and Boom.

"Your turn," said Woolverton.

Boom rolled the ball of wool to Shirelle, who rolled it to Lillian, who rolled it to Lionel, and so on until everyone was touching a piece of wool. Finally, when the ball rolled back to Woolverton, Daisy saw that the wool had made a pattern in the snow and that everyone was linked to everyone else.

"It's beautiful," said Daisy.

"It's a web of friendship," said Shirelle.

"To catch you if you fall."

Later, when Daisy was warm in bed again and drifting off to sleep, she heard the sheep singing softly as they wandered back to the fields. She wondered what her mom would make of all the patterns and hoofprints in the backyard. But the next morning when she woke, a fresh snowfall had completely covered the lawn in a blanket of white.

As she walked to school on Monday
morning, Daisy was surprised to see
Woolverton running across the fields
toward her.

"Hello, Woolverton," she said as he
reached the gate. "Off exploring again?"
Woolverton, who had been carrying
something in his mouth, dropped it in the

snow and pushed it under the gate with his nose.

"I forgot to give you this," he said. "I made it myself."

Daisy bent down to pick it up and saw that it was a small ball of wool. "Thanks, Woolverton," she said. "What's it for?"

"It's in case you ever decide to go off and see the world," Woolverton explained. "Before you leave, just tie one end to a tree. Then when you want to come home again, it'll help you find your way back."

"Gosh," said Daisy. "It must be a very long ball of wool."

"Not really," said Woolverton. "I don't want you to go very far away."

Daisy smiled and stroked the top of his head. "I won't," she said. "Not just yet, anyway."

The sound of bleating floated through the air, and Woolverton jumped up and ran back across the fields, disappearing over the hill.

Daisy looked up and saw that Boom was waiting for her in the lane.

"Boom," she said as they walked toward school, "do you think I'll go off and see the world one day?"

"Almost certainly," said Boom.

"Oh," said Daisy. She was quiet for a moment or two. Then she asked, "Will you mind very much?"

"Probably," he said. "For a while, at least. But then I'll just think about Shirelle and Ricky and that will make me feel better."

Daisy frowned. "I don't understand."

Boom stopped and looked up at her. "Shirelle and Ricky both lost something, remember? But in the end it came back to them, didn't it? It came back."

Daisy smiled and put her arms around his neck. "And so will I," she whispered. Then she kissed him and ran away toward the

gates of
Nettlegreen
Elementary School, the
ball of wool clutched tightly
in the palm of her hand.